W9-ARV-309

The Buddy Files

THE CASE OF THE
SCHOOL
GHOST

Dori Hillestad Butler

Pictures by Jeremy Tugeau

Albert Whitman & Company
Chicago, Illinois

Library of Congress Cataloging-in-Publication Data

Butler, Dori Hillestad.
The Buddy files : the case of the school ghost / by Dori Hillestad Butler ; illustrated
by Jeremy Tugeau.
p. cm.
Summary: When therapy dog Buddy attends the fourth grade
sleepover in the school's library, he solves the mystery of the school ghost.
ISBN 978-0-8075-0915-9 (hardcover)
[1. Dogs—Fiction. 2. Schools—Fiction. 3. Sleepovers—Fiction. 4. Mystery and
detective stories.] I. Tugeau, Jeremy, ill. II. Title. III. Title: Case of the school ghost.
PZ7.B9759Bur 2010
[Fic]—dc23
2011016025

The design is by Nick Tiemersma.

For more information about Albert Whitman & Company,
visit our web site at www.albertwhitman.com.

For Michelle.
Thank you for all you've
done for Buddy...and for me.

Table of Contents

1
Message from Agatha

Hello!

My name is Buddy. I'm a therapy dog. That means I go to school and help kids. Sometimes I help them with reading. Sometimes I help them solve problems. Sometimes I just put my head in their laps and let them pet me. Petting a dog helps

humans feel better when they are upset. I LOVE being a therapy dog. It's my favorite job!

I have another favorite job besides therapy dog. I'm also a detective. I've solved a bunch of cases already: the Case of the Lost Boy, the Case of the Mixed-up Mutts, the Case of the Missing Family, the Case of the Fire Alarm, and the Case of the Library Monster.

Here's a case I haven't solved yet: the Case of the School Ghost.

A lot of humans and animals think there's a ghost at Four Lakes Elementary School. I don't know if there's a ghost there or not. I don't even know if I believe in ghosts.

Here's one thing I DO know:

🐾 Some strange things have happened at that school.

Here's a list of some of the strange things I've seen, heard, and felt there:

🐾 Doors closing all by themselves.
🐾 Lights flickering and going out all by themselves.
🐾 Noises in the walls and the ceiling.
🐾 Cold air rippling through my fur. Like a GHOST is trying to pet me!

Maybe tonight I will solve the Case of the School Ghost once and for all, because guess what? I GET TO GO

TO A SLEEPOVER WITH CONNOR
AT SCHOOL TONIGHT! We're going
to stay all night and sleep in sleeping
bags in the library. It's going to be so
fun!

The sleepover is for fourth graders
who have read five hundred pages
so far this school year. I'm not a
fourth grader. And I haven't read five
hundred pages. But Mom is the alpha
human at school. If she says I can go
to the sleepover, then I can go to the
sleepover.

Right now I am lying on the floor
by Connor's bed, watching him pack.

"Shirt, pants, underwear, socks,
pajamas," Connor says. "Is that
everything, Buddy?"

"What about food?" I ask. "And

your bowls? And some toys?" That's what we bring for me when I go someplace and stay overnight. Food, my bowls, and some toys. I don't need any of that other stuff that Connor is packing.

Connor slaps the side of his head. "I almost forgot my toothbrush." He dashes out of the room.

I wouldn't mind if Mom and Connor forgot my toothbrush. I HATE having my teeth brushed.

Hey, maybe I should see what Mom packed for me. If she packed my toothbrush, there's still time to hide it under the refrigerator. Or in the garbage can.

I trot down the hall and down the stairs. There's a paper bag on the

floor in the kitchen. Sniff…sniff…
I smell my FOOD! I stick my nose
inside the bag. The bag topples over
and everything inside spills out. A
bag of food, a bag of liver treats, my
bowls, my leash, my ball, and my
squeaky duck. I LOVE my squeaky
duck. It's my favorite toy!

"Buddy!" Mom cries.

My heart jumps inside my chest.
"Oh, hi, Mom," I say with my tail. "I
didn't hear you come up behind me."
Mom stuffs everything, including the
duck, back inside the bag. She makes
mad eyes at me and blows a bunch of
air out through her mouth.

"What?" I say. "What did I do?"

Mom doesn't tell me.

I think I'll go outside for a little

bit. Maybe when I get back Mom will be in a better mood.

I charge through my doggy door, across the back porch, and down into the yard. Sniff... sniff... the air smells heavy and wet. The sky is growing dark. It feels like it might storm soon.

I circle the yard, searching for the perfect spot to do my business. Someplace where I haven't gone in a while, but not too far from where I normally go. Ah, here's a good spot. I lift my leg and... all of a sudden I have the feeling I'm being watched. I glance over my shoulder, but I don't see anyone . I finish my business, then turn all around. I see our big tree, some flowers, the tall fence. I don't see any intruders.

Then I look up. Above the fence. Cat with No Name has draped himself across a tree branch that's hanging partway into our yard.

"Why do you always have to sneak up on me?" I ask.

"I didn't sneak," Cat says. "I've been here all afternoon."

"Why?" I ask. Doesn't he have anything better to do than watch my backyard? It's my job to watch my backyard, not his.

Cat licks his front paw. "I was waiting for you to come outside," he says. "I have a message for you."

A message? For me?

"From who?" I ask, padding over to the fence.

"Agatha," Cat says.

Agatha is the name of the ghost at school. If there really is a ghost at school.

I swallow hard. "What's the message?"

"Stay out of the basement," Cat says. "Agatha doesn't like people or animals hanging around her school at night. She won't bother you if you keep everyone out of the basement. But if you, or anyone else, goes down there tonight, you'll be sorry."

I don't know if Cat is messing with me or not.

"What do you mean?" I ask. "What'll happen if I go down there? What'll happen if any of the kids go down there?"

"You don't want to know," Cat

says. "But trust me. It'll be bad."

The sleepover is going to be in the library, so I don't think anyone will want to go to the basement.

But I could be wrong.

2
Agatha's Story

I follow Mom and Connor back and forth from the house to the garage. Back to the house. Back to the garage. House. Garage. They are loading suitcases and boxes and grocery bags into the car. I think this is all the stuff we are bringing to the sleepover.

"Don't forget the bag with my food in it," I tell Mom and Connor. I go over to show them which bag I'm talking about. But they each grab different bags.

"Um, guys? My food?" I say again. Finally, Mom picks up the bag with my food. I wag my tail and start to follow her back out to the car.

Ding! Dong!

"I'll get it," Connor says, racing for the front door. I think I can trust Mom to put my food in the car by herself, so I hurry after Connor. I can't wait to see who's here!

But when Connor opens the front door, nobody is here.

There's a box sitting on the front porch, though. Thunder rumbles in the distance as Conner and I step outside. We both gaze around the front yard, and up and down the block, but there is nobody around. I lunge for the box. Sniff…sniff…sniff. I can't tell what's inside. I can't tell who sent it, either. Somebody we don't know.

Connor opens the box. Inside is a flashlight and two pieces of paper. One. Two.

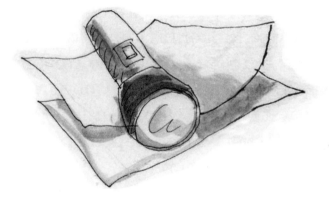

I smell chocolate and bubblegum on the box, the flashlight, and the papers.

"What do those papers say?" I ask as Connor reads one to himself.

"Hmm," he says. His eyebrows scrunch together and he flips to the other paper.

I peer over his arm. There are a lot of words on those papers. I know some of them: *who, you, are, she, has,* and *a*. Mrs. Warner says those are "sight words." Sight words are words you know when you see them. Most of the words on Connor's paper are not sight words.

"Let's go, Connor," Mom calls from the garage.

"Coming!" Connor calls back.

We go inside and Connor stuffs the flashlight and the papers into his suitcase. Then we go out to the car.

We pick up Connor's friend Michael on the way to school. Too bad my friend Mouse doesn't get to come, too. Mouse is a dog, not a mouse. He is the biggest, loudest dog on our street. He lives at Michael's house. But he lives outside the house and Michael lives inside the house.

I feel sad that Mouse doesn't get to come to the sleepover.

"IT'S OKAY, BUDDY," Mouse says. "KEEP AN EYE ON MY BOY WHILE HE'S GONE." Mouse is so big that he can't help yelling when he talks.

"I will," I promise Mouse.

Michael climbs into the backseat with me and Connor. And then we are off to school. I LOVE school. It's my favorite place!

Connor and Michael don't say much in the car. Usually Connor and Michael have a lot to say to each other. But today they are both very quiet.

Then I notice Michael's backpack. There's a flashlight sticking out of one of the pockets. Sniff... sniff... This flashlight has the same chocolate and bubblegum scent on it as the flashlight and papers that Connor found in the box outside our house!

Connor notices Michael's flashlight soon after I do. "Hey, I have a flashlight like that," he says.

"Yeah?" Michael says. "I, um, just got it. Today."

"Did you find it in a box on your

front porch?" I ask Michael.

Michael doesn't answer me.

"I...just got mine today, too," Connor says.

The boys look at each other. They both look like they want to say something more, but neither one does. Finally, they sit back and watch the rain fall outside their windows.

Why don't they say more about those flashlights? I wonder. I want to know where the flashlights came from.

Who would ring a doorbell, leave a flashlight and some papers in a box by the door, and then run away? Even more important, why would someone do that?

Hmm. I think I have a new case to solve.

When we get to school, Connor and Michael help Mom carry things into the school. They move fast because it's pouring outside.

They bring everything to the library and Mrs. Warner shows them where to put it. Mom may be the boss of the school, but Mrs. Warner is the boss of the library.

I greet all the kids as they arrive. Most of them give me a pat or a hug. They all come in soaking wet, but so, so, so excited. I'm excited, too!

The kids unroll their sleeping bags, talk, laugh, and run around. It's getting very, very loud in the library, but tonight Mrs. Warner doesn't seem to mind.

Then Mr. Poe comes. Mr. Poe always smells so interesting because he does a lot of different jobs at the school. Today he smells like PIZZA!

"Pizza's here!" Mr. Poe says. "It's in the cafeteria."

"Yay, pizza!" several kids cry as they charge for the door.

I know how they feel. I LOVE pizza. It's my favorite food!

I race down the hall with all the kids. When we get to the cafeteria, we crowd around a table that has about twelve or nine pizzas on it. Sniff... sniff... I smell tomatoes... cheese... crust...

pepperoni ... sausage ... more cheese ... onions ... mushrooms. I LOVE all that stuff!

"Not for you, Buddy," Connor shoves my nose away from the table.

Darn. The good stuff is never for me.

Oh well. There are pizza crumbs on the floor. I clean them up as I follow Connor and Michael over to one of the long tables.

Kids greet me along the way. "Hi, Buddy!" "Hey, Buddy!" "How are you doing, Buddy?" One even slips me his pizza crust.

"Thank you!" I say, licking my lips.

Rain pounds against the roof above the cafeteria. Lightning flashes.

Thunder crashes. Several kids jump.
Sniff...sniff...I smell scared kids.

"It's okay," I say to all the kids.
"It's just a little thunderstorm."

"Aw!" A girl who smells like sausage and flowers turns around and hugs me. "Buddy's scared of the storm."

What? No, I'm not. "You're the one who's scared. Not me," I say, licking her cheek. Maybe if she pets me she won't feel so scared.

All of a sudden there is a strange banging sound above us. Like someone is up there pounding on the ceiling with a hammer. The cafeteria grows quiet and everyone looks up. But the noise stops almost as suddenly as it began.

Everyone goes back to what they were doing. Eating...talking...or in my case, cleaning up pizza crumbs on the floor.

There are A LOT of crumbs under the table. I squeeze in between all the legs and feet. It's dark under here, but I don't need light to find crumbs. Hey, there's part of an actual piece of pizza. I pounce on it and gobble it up. YUM!!!!!

My nose twitches. I smell something in the bag under that chair. It's not pizza. In fact, it's not food at all. But there's something very interesting in that bag. Something I've smelled recently.

I bite at the string on the bag

and the bag loosens enough for me to stick my nose inside. There's another flashlight in here. A flashlight that looks and smells like Connor's and Michael's flashlights.

"What are you doing under there, Buddy?" Jillian asks, grabbing the bag away from me.

Hey, I know Jillian! She was Kayla's friend. Kayla was my human before Connor.

"Is that your flashlight?" I ask Jillian, resting my head on her knee. "Where did you get it?"

She gives me a quick pat on the head, then tightens the string on her bag without answering me.

Thunder crashes again. This time the lights above us flicker. The banging in the ceiling starts again.

"What is that noise?" a boy who smells like three different dogs asks.

"I don't think Agatha likes the storm," Mr. Poe says as he sweeps the floor behind a boy who smells like pepperoni, fish, and frogs.

"Is Agatha making that noise? Is Agatha making the lights blink?" Jillian asks.

"I don't know who else could be doing it," Mr. Poe says.

"Do you think we'll see Agatha tonight?" Dog Boy asks. He sounds like he wants to see Agatha.

"Maybe," Mr. Poe says with a twinkle in his eye. "I've heard she likes to come out during the fourth grade sleepover."

"Ooooooooo!" a bunch of kids cry in delight.

"Tell us the story of Agatha, Mr. Poe," the girl near Dog Boy says.

"Yeah, tell us!" Pepperoni-Fish-Frog Boy says.

Mr. Poe grins. "I think you all know the story of Agatha," he says, swishing the broom left and right.

"Tell us anyway!" several kids say at once.

Mr. Poe checks his watch. "All right. I'll give you the short version."

Jillian grabs her bag and gets up to leave. I know I should follow her if I want to solve the Case of the Flashlights. But I also want to solve the Case of the School Ghost.

I crawl out from under the bench,

lie down, and listen to Mr. Poe.

"Agatha was a girl who went to school here a long, long time ago," Mr. Poe says, leaning on his broom. "She'd been in a fire when she was a young girl, so her face was scarred. Some of the kids made fun of her. In fact, a lot of kids made fun of her."

I never heard that part of the story before.

"That made her sad when she was a little girl," Mr. Poe goes on.

It makes me sad, too.

"And it made her mad when she was an old woman," Mr. Poe says. "Agatha always remembered how badly kids treated her in school. So after she died, her ghost returned to her old school. This school. And she still haunts the school to this very day."

"Have you ever seen Agatha, Mr. Poe?" the girl next to Dog Boy asks.

"Mr. Poe!" Mom cuts him off. Her hands are on her hips. "Are you trying to scare these kids out of their wits? There are no such things as ghosts. You know that. This is an old building. Things moan and creak. Sometimes we have trouble with the electricity. That loud banging is the hot water pipes. There are no ghosts here."

When Mom walks away, Mr. Poe leans over the table and whispers, "That's what Agatha wants us to think."

3
A Ghostly Warning!

I wish I knew whether there really were such things as ghosts. I wish I knew whether there was a ghost at this school.

Whenever I want to solve a mystery like this, I start by making lists inside my head. Lists help me keep track of what I know and what I don't know. They also help me make a plan.

Here is what I know about Agatha:

- 🐾 She went to school here a long, long time ago.
- 🐾 She isn't alive anymore.

Here is what I don't know about Agatha:

- 🐾 Is she really a ghost?
- 🐾 Did she make the lights flicker?
- 🐾 Is she banging around in the ceiling?

I know a lot of humans and animals who say they've seen Agatha. But I don't know if any of them have really seen her. Sometimes humans

think they've seen a ghost when
they've really seen something else.
Sometimes humans even lie about
seeing ghosts. I don't know why they
do that.

Cat with No Name says he sees
and talks to Agatha all the time. But
you can't believe everything a cat
tells you.

You can believe dogs, though.
Dogs never lie.

I know a dog who says she's seen
Agatha. The dog's name is Jazzy and
she lives right behind the school. I
don't know if Jazzy really saw a ghost
or if she just thinks she saw a ghost.
She definitely saw something, though.
And I'm going to find out what.

Here is my plan:

🐾 Stay up all night and watch for ghosts!

I don't know what I'll do if I actually see one.

"Gather round, everyone." Mrs. Warner claps her hands together as the storm rages outside. We are in the library now. "It's time for the scavenger hunt!"

Oh, boy! A scavenger hunt! I LOVE scavenger hunts. They're my favorite—wait. What's a scavenger hunt?

Whatever it is, it must be fun because all the kids go zooming over to Mrs. Warner. They smell excited.

So I zoom over, too. I nose my way into the circle between Connor and Michael.

Mrs. Warner holds up some papers. I sniff them. They don't smell like the papers Connor found in the box with the flashlight.

"Each group will get a list of things to find around the school," Mrs. Warner explains. "The first group that finds everything on their list is the winner."

I wag my tail. I'm good at finding things.

"Can we pick our own groups?" Michael asks.

"No, we're going to number off," Mrs. Warner says. She points to each kid and says a number.

I sit up extra tall so Mrs. Warner sees me. But she doesn't give me a number.

"Okay," Mrs. Warner says. "Ones over here. Twos over there. Threes over there. And fours over there."

"Whichever group finds all the items on their list first wins the scavenger hunt," Mrs. Warner says. "Are you ready? Go!"

Go? I don't know where to go. I see Connor and some girls hunched over their paper. I scamper over to them.

A girl who smells like pizza, cats, and nail polish reads from the paper. "A straw, a pink bead, a white rock, a left mitten, a lock of red hair, a book told from a dog's point of view." She looks up at the others in the group. "Where are we supposed to find all this stuff?"

"We can find the book here," another girl who smells like pizza and different nail polish says. "Who knows a dog book?"

"*Shiloh*!" the first girl says.

Connor says, "That's told from a boy's point of view, not a dog's point of view."

"How are we supposed to find one from a dog's point of view?" the second nail polish girl says.

"Aaaaaaaaaaa!" someone shrieks from the far book shelf. Several boys and girls run out from those shelves. "Mrs. Warner! Mrs. Warner!" they all cry. "There's a ghost back there!"

What? Really?

"There are no such things as ghosts," Mrs. Warner says.

"Yes, there are," one of the girls insists. "We all heard it. It said, 'Staaaaay out of the baaasement,'" That's the same as the message I got from Cat with No Name.

I hurry over to where all those kids came from. If Agatha is back in those book shelves, I want to meet her. I want to talk to her. A bunch of kids and Mrs. Warner all follow me. Halfway down the aisle, I hear the ghostly voice, too. "Staaaaay out of the baaasement."

Sniff... sniff... I smell something behind those books.

The last time I smelled something

behind some books in the library, it was a blue-tongued skink! My friend Maya hid him and some other lizards in the school basement, but then he got loose! I found him in the library, but he escaped before any of the humans found him. It took a long, long, long, long time to find him after that. Now he lives in a glass cage behind Mrs. Warner's desk. His name is Fluffy, but I call him Blue Tongue. Whatever is back there today, it doesn't smell like a blue-tongued skink. Whatever it is smells dusty and electrical. It's making sort of a scratchy, whispery noise.

I stand up on my hind legs and nose some of the books out of the way.

"What's Buddy doing?" one of the

girls asks.

"Mrs. Warner," another girl says. "Buddy's knocking books on the floor."

"He probably smells something," Connor says.

"I do! I smell—hmm. What is that thing on the shelf?" Some sort of metal box. It's small, so I pick it up with my mouth.

"What is it?" a girl asks. "What does Buddy have?"

Connor takes the box from me. It starts talking in Connor's hand. "Staaaaay out of the baaasement."

"It's an old tape recorder," one of the girls says.

Mrs. Warner holds out her hand and Connor gives her the

tape recorder. Mrs. Warner presses a button on the recorder. There's a loud click and the whispery noise stops.

"Whose is this?" Mrs. Warner asks.

All the kids look at each other, but no one raises a hand.

I sniff the recorder. It's has Jillian's scent all over it.

I turn to Jillian, but she is looking at the ceiling. Why doesn't she tell Mrs. Warner that the recorder is hers?

Why would Jillian hide a tape recorder behind the books? Does she want people to think there's a ghost in the library? Is she trying to scare people? Why would she do that?

"Fine. I'll just keep this until someone claims it," Mrs. Warner says. She brings the recorder over to her desk and puts it in the top drawer.

4
Why Is Everyone Acting So Weird?

After the scavenger hunt is over, the kids scatter to different parts of the school. Some stay in the library and read or play board games. Others go to the gym. I follow Connor to the art room.

On most days, Mrs. Sobol is the alpha human in the art room. But she's not here tonight.

Mom was here a little while ago. She set out some paper, pencils, and paints, but then she went to check on the kids in the gym. I don't think there is an alpha human in the art room right now.

I guess that means I'm in charge.

I stroll around the tables and glance at everyone's artwork. Michael is painting a school with ghosts coming out of it. A girl who smells like chocolate and mints is drawing the girl beside her. Connor is hunched over his paper, so it's hard to see what he's drawing. But I nudge my nose in anyway. It looks like letters. Just letters. No picture. A...B...C...D...E...F...G...H... I...J...K...L...M...N...O...P... Q...R...S...T...U...V...W...X... Y...Z.

That's weird.

Do those letters spell any words when they're spread out all over the paper like that?

Connor picks up his paper and walks over to the window. He peers out into the darkness. What? Is there something out there? I go over to the window and look. All I see is rain pouring down.

Connor grabs an empty jar from the shelf below the window, hides it under his paper, and scurries over to the door. He is acting very strange.

"Hey!" I say, trotting after him. "Where are you going?" The door starts to close on my face, but I push it back open.

"Connor, wait up!" I follow him

down the hall.

Connor turns when he hears me. "Go back to the art room, Buddy," he says in a low voice.

"No!" I say. "I want to know where you're going."

"Or go find Mom," Connor says. I sit. I'm not going anywhere.

Connor sighs. "Okay. But if you're coming with me, then you have to be quiet."

I can be quiet. But I wish Connor would tell me where we're going and why he's acting so strange.

We turn down another hall. A dark one. We tiptoe past one … two … seven more doors until we reach the music room. Connor's eyes dart back and forth, then he

turns the doorknob. The door creaks open and we slip inside.

It's even darker in here than it was in the hallway, but Connor doesn't turn on the light.

He's about to bump into a table, so I nudge him out of the way. Lightning flashes and lights up the room. Connor shuffles over to the piano and sets the empty jar and the paper on top. Then we leave.

"Why did you put that jar and paper on the piano?" I ask as Connor closes the door behind us.

Connor doesn't answer.

We walk back down the dark hall.

As we go around a corner, Connor almost crashes into Michael.

"There you are!" Michael says.

"Where were you? We've been looking for you. A bunch of us are choosing up for basketball. Do you want to play?"

Oh, boy! Basketball. I LOVE basketball. It's my favorite sport!

"Sure," Connor says. "Let's go!"

Yeah, let's go! I follow Connor and Michael down the main stairs to the gym.

Pepperoni-Fish-Frog Boy and Dog Boy are choosing teams. I run back and forth between them saying, "Pick me! Pick me!" But neither of them does.

Oh well. I'll play on both teams.

I race up and down the gym, chasing the ball. "Mine!" I say, jumping up and grabbing it away

from some kid. But I can't hang onto
the ball very well with my paws. It
rolls to the side of the gym.

"Buddy!" someone yells at me.

"Sorry," I say.

Connor jogs after the ball. He
tosses it to Pepperoni-Fish-Frog Boy
and the game starts again. I see out
the corner of my eye that Michael
is leaving. Why is he leaving in the
middle of the game? Maybe he needs
to go outside.

I dart in between kids and grab
for the ball. But once again it slips
through my paws and rolls away.

"Buddy!" several kids yell at me
now.

"Sorry!" I say. I'm doing the best
I can.

"Maybe you should take your dog back to the library, Connor," Pepperoni-Fish-Frog Boy says. "He keeps getting in the way."

What? No!

"Okay," Connor says. "Come on, Buddy." He grabs me by the collar.

"That's not fair!" I cry. "I'm not the only one who can't hang onto the ball. Why do I have to stop playing?"

But before Connor can answer me we hear a shriek from somewhere outside the gym. It sounds like Michael.

"Michael?" I call, tearing out of the gym. I run up the stairs and around the corner to where I heard the shrieking. A bunch of kids follow me.

"There's a ghost in the music

room!" Michael cries, his eyes wide.
He is standing in front of the door
to the music room. Some of the kids
press their noses to the window and
peer inside.

"I don't see any ghost," says
Pepperoni-Fish-Frog Boy.

"Neither do I," says Dog Boy.

I force myself in between them.
There was no ghost when Connor
and I were in there five or fifty
minutes ago. I sniff all around the
door. I don't smell anything unusual.
The kids all want to know more
about the ghost. "What kind of ghost
did you see?" "What did it look like?"
"What did it do?" "Was it Agatha?"
they ask.

"I don't know if it was Agatha,

but it was definitely a girl ghost," Michael says. "She was out here in the hall at first, just sort of floating around. Then she went into the music room. She went right through the wall. Then she disappeared."

"Wow," says one of the kids as thunder crashes above us.

There's only one problem with Michael's story. It's not true.
I can see and smell the lie all over Michael.

Mom makes her way through the crowd. "Kids, listen to me," she says. "There are no such things as ghosts. I think this storm is causing your imaginations to run away with you."

"It wasn't my imagination," Michael insists.

"Well, regardless of what you saw, I want you to stay away from the music room," Mom says. "That goes for all of you. We're going to start a movie in the library in about half an hour. You can be in the library, the art room, or the gym until then. But please don't go running around the school. Okay?"

Everyone agrees, and Mom turns back toward the library.

"I really did see a ghost," Michael says in a low voice. "I know I did."

But he's still lying.

Why would Michael say he saw a ghost when he didn't?

Why would Connor sneak an empty jar and a big piece of paper into the music room?

59

And why would Jillian hide a tape recorder with a ghostly voice behind some books?

Have all the kids in this school gone crazy?

5
Comparing Notes

I am lying half on Connor's sleeping bag and half on Michael's sleeping bag. The lights above are dim. A movie is playing on the TV. Rain pounds against the library windows.

Connor and Michael both seem kind of restless. I don't think either one of them is enjoying the movie very much. I don't blame them; there are no dogs in this movie.

Across the library, I see Jillian

get up and tiptoe around all the
sleeping bags.

A little while later, Michael leans
over and whispers to Connor, "I have to
go to the bathroom. Will you tell your
mom if she wonders where I'm at?"

"Sure," Connor says.

But soon after that Connor gets up
and heads for the door.

"Where are we going, Connor?" I
ask, trailing after him. "Are we going
to the bathroom like Michael?"

"Do you have to go everywhere I go,
Buddy?" Connor asks when we are in
the bright hallway outside the library.

I think about that for a few
seconds. "Yes," I say. "You're my
human!"

It turns out we aren't going to the

bathroom. We are headed toward that dark, dark hallway again. The one where the music room is.

I stop. "Didn't Mom say we should stay away from the music room?"

Connor keeps walking. All the way to the music room. I don't want to get left behind, so I run to catch up. Even though I'm not sure we should be here.

Connor cracks the door open and we slip inside. Again. But this time we're not the only ones here. Michael and Jillian are here, too. They are sitting on the floor by the piano, waving lit flashlights around the dark room. I run over to greet them.

"Hi, Buddy," they both say, petting me.

Connor closes the door. "What are you guys doing here?" he asks.

"Probably the same thing you're doing here," Jillian says.

"Did you get a letter that said come to the music room at 9:15?" Michael asks.

"Yes," Connor says.

"I knew it!" Michael grins at Connor. "When you said you had a flashlight like mine, and you just got it today, I knew you got a letter, too."

Connor sits down next to Michael and Jillian. "Why didn't you say so?" Connor asks.

"Why didn't you?" Michael asks.

Jillian rolls her eyes. "The letters said, "Don't tell ANYONE,'" Jillian says, holding up a piece of paper. "At least that's what mine says."

"Can I see your letter?" Connor asks.

Jillian hands him her paper. "Can I see yours?" she asks.

"Why don't we all read our letters out loud?" Michael suggests.

I wag my tail. I like that idea.

"Okay," Connor says. He hands Jillian's letter back to her, then pulls a paper out of his pocket.

"I'll read mine first," Michael says, holding his flashlight over the paper. "'Dear Michael. Agatha knows who you are. She has chosen you for a special job.

"*Step 1: At exactly 8:35 p.m. stop whatever you're doing and go to the music room. Don't let anyone follow you. Once you're there, act like you saw a ghost in the music room. Be convincing!*

   "**Step 2:** *At exactly 9:15 p.m. come back to the music room. Bring this flashlight. Wait in the music room for more directions.* **Warning:** *Don't tell ANYONE you received this letter ... or else!*"

   So that's why Michael lied about seeing a ghost earlier.

   "Okay, I'll read mine next," Jillian says. "'Dear Jillian. Agatha knows who you are. She has chosen you for a special job.

   "**Step 1:** *Find a tape recorder and make a thirty minute tape of a ghostly voice. The voice should say over and over again, 'Stay out of the basement.' Right before the scavenger hunt starts,*

hide your recorder in the library and turn it on. Don't let anyone see you.

"**Step 2:** *At exactly 9:15 p.m. come to the music room. Bring this flashlight. Wait in the music room for more directions.* **Warning:** *Don't tell ANYBODY you received this letter … or else!*'"

And that's why Jillian hid a tape recorder with ghostly sounds in the library.

Jillian tosses the paper down in front of her. "That was my mom's tape recorder. Do you know how much trouble I'm going to be in if I don't get it back from Mrs. Warner?"

"You'll get it back," Connor says. "All you have to do is tell Mrs. Warner it's yours."

"Yeah, and then I'll get in trouble with Mrs. Warner," Jillian says. "She may even tell my mom what I did with the recorder. I'm in trouble no matter what."

I'm not sure I like the person who sent these letters. He or she is getting my friends in trouble.

"Both your letters tell you to wait in the music room for more directions," Connor says. "My letter has more directions."

"Really?" Jillian says.

"What does your letter say, Connor?" Michael asks.

Connor adjusts his flashlight and reads, "Dear Connor. Agatha knows who you are. She has chosen you for a special job.

"*Step 1: Go to the art room at exactly 8:05 p.m. Grab an empty jar and a large piece of paper. Write the alphabet on the paper. Leave lots of room between letters. Then take those things to the music room. Don't let anyone see you.*

"*Step 2: At exactly 9:15 p.m. come to the music room. Bring this flashlight.*

"*Step 3: Once everyone is there,*

*have them sit in a circle. Put the paper
and jar in the center. Have everyone
put two fingers on the jar. Then tell
Agatha you are ready. Her spirit will
enter the jar. Your fingers will give
her strength. With your help, she will
move the jar over the letters and spell
out her message to you.* **Warning:**
*Don't tell ANYBODY you received this
letter...or else!"*

That's why Connor snuck a jar and
piece of paper into the music room.

"Wow, we're going to get to talk to
Agatha?" Michael says. "For real?"

"With a jar?" Jillian asks. "How is
that going to work? If Agatha is really
here, why doesn't she just talk to us?
Why does she need a jar and a paper
with letters?"

"Have you ever talked to a ghost before?" Michael asks. "Maybe this is how they talk to people."

"Or maybe she thought it would be more fun to talk to us this way," Connor says.

"Hey, weren't there two letters in that box with the flashlight?" I ask Connor. "I counted them. One. Two. You should read the other letter to us, too."

But I don't think Connor understands me.

"Does anybody have any idea who sent these letters to us?" Jillian asks.

"No," Connor says.

Michael shakes his head.

I want to know who sent those letters, too. In fact, there are a lot of things I want to know about those letters. For instance:

- 🐾 Does the person who sent the letters really know Agatha?
- 🐾 Why were the letters sent to Connor, Michael, and Jillian? Why did Agatha choose them for some special jobs?
- 🐾 Did anyone else get a letter?
- 🐾 Why did Connor, Michael, and Jillian do what these letters told them to do when they don't even know who sent the letters? Especially when some of these things could get them in trouble?

🐾 What does Connor's other letter say?

"Did you do what the letter said?" Michael asks Connor. "Did you get a piece of paper and a jar? And did you write the alphabet on the paper?"

"Yes. It's over there." Connor points to the piano.

Michael goes over and grabs the paper and jar. "Maybe we should do what Connor's letter says."

"I don't know," I say. "I think we should find out who sent the letters. We don't want any more trouble."

But of course, no one pays attention to the dog.

"All right," Jillian says. "Let's see if we can talk to a ghost."

6
Agatha Speaks

Michael lays the paper on the floor. Connor starts to set the jar down, but then pulls it back. "The letter didn't say where to put the jar," he says.

"It doesn't matter. Put it anywhere," Michael says.

Connor sets it on some letters in the middle of the page.

Connor, Michael, and Jillian lay

their flashlights in their lap. Then they all scoot in closer and place their fingers on the jar.

"What do we do now?" Michael asks.

"We tell Agatha we're ready," Connor says.

"Okay," Jillian says. "How do we do that?"

Connor shrugs. "I think we just call her name or something." He clears his throat, then says, "Agatha? Oh, Agatha! We're here. Are you here, too?" He looks around the dark room.

The jar on the paper starts to move.

Michael's eyes grow wide. "Are you guys doing that?"

"No," Jillian says. "I'm barely touching it. See?" She takes her fingers off the jar.

Connor lifts his fingers, too. "Same here."

I inch a little closer so I can sniff the jar. I smell paint … and soap … and mayo. No ghosts.

"Off the paper, Buddy," Connor says, shoving me with his elbow.

"I'm just trying to help," I say. But I back up, lay down, and rest my head on my paws.

The jar stops over a letter. "I," Jillian says.

Then the jar slides to another letter. "M," Jillian says.

Connor and Michael say the next letters with Jillian. "H ... E ... R ... E." "Without the apostrophe that spells out 'I'm here.'" Michael says.

Jillian pulls her fingers away like the jar is on fire. "Is that really Agatha?" she whispers.

"Put your fingers back on," Connor says. "It's moving again."

Jillian returns her fingers to the jar and the jar sails across more letters.   This time Connor

says the words as they appear.
"Yes ... it's ... really ... me."

"I think one of you is moving the jar," Jillian says.

"I'm not! I swear," Michael insists.

He smells like he's telling the truth.

"I'm not, either," Connor says.

I sit back up. I think I smell a lie on Connor.

"Somebody ask Connor another question," I say. "Or ask him the same question. Ask him if he's moving the jar." My boy doesn't lie very often. Maybe I'm smelling something else on Connor. Something that smells like a lie, but really isn't.

"Stop barking, Buddy," Connor says.

"Maybe he's barking because he sees Agatha," Michael says. "Everyone knows dogs can see things that we can't."

"No, I don't see Agatha," I say. "I—"

"Shh, Buddy!" Connor says again.

I lay back down. I don't like it when Connor shushes me. And I really don't like it when I smell a lie on him.

"Okay, Agatha," Connor says, staring at the jar. "Do you have a message for us?"

"Y … E … S," Connor reads.

"What's the message?" Michael asks.

Connor, Michael and Jillian peer over the jar as it starts to move

again. "G...O...T...O...T...H...E...
F...U...R—"

"Wait. Got...what?" Jillian says.
"The jar is moving too fast."

"The first word isn't 'got,'" Connor
says. "It's 'go.' Go to the...something."

"Are you sure?" Michael asks. "I
thought it was 'got,' too. 'Got other'
something."

The jar stops.

I have no idea what words the jar
is spelling.

"Maybe one of us should write
down the letters the jar stops on,"
Jillian suggests.

"Would that work?" Michael asks.
"The directions say we all have to put
two fingers on the jar."

"Let's ask Agatha," Connor says.

He turns to the jar. "Agatha, is it okay if only two of us have our fingers on the jar? That way one of us can write down the message."

The kids place their fingers back on the rim of the jar. "Y ... E ... S."

Jillian shines the flashlight around the room. "Hey, there's a chalkboard," she says, hopping to her feet. She goes over to the chalkboard. "You guys read the letters to me and I'll write them down," Jillian says, holding her flashlight in one hand and a piece of chalk in the other.

"Okay," Connor and Michael say at the same time.

Michael turns to the jar.

"We're ready, Agatha," he says. "Tell us your message." The jar glides across the paper. Whenever it stops for a few seconds, Michael and Connor call out a letter and Jillian writes it down:

"G...O...T...O...T...H...E... F...U...R...N...A...C...E...R... O...O...M."

"I think that's it," Connor says. The jar remains still.

Jillian shines her flashlight across the message. She draws lines between some of the letters. "Go to the furnace room," she reads. She turns to the boys. "Why do we have to go to the furnace room?"

Furnace room? I know about the furnace room. That's where Maya hid Blue Tongue and his friends twenty or four days ago.

"The jar's moving again," Connor says. Michael reads: "Y...O...U... W...I...L...L...F...I...N...D... O...U...T...W...H...E...N...Y... O...U...G...E...T...T...H...E... R...E."

Jillian draws more lines, then puts it all together. "You will find out when you get there."

"Do you have any other messages for us?" Connor asks the jar.

"N...O."

"I don't even know where the furnace room is," Michael says. "Do you guys?"

"I think it's in the basement," Connor says.

7
Lights Out!

CRACK! BOOM! Connor, Michael, Jillian and I all just about jump out of our skins.

That was one of the brightest lightning flashes I've ever seen and one of the loudest thunder crashes I've ever heard. It shook the whole school.

"I—I...wonder if we should go back to the library," Connor says in a shaky voice.

"We can't go back yet," Michael

says. "We have to do what Agatha says. We have to go to the furnace room."

But the furnace room is in the basement. And Cat with No Name told me that Agatha wants me to keep everyone out of the basement. He said Agatha doesn't like people hanging around her school at night, and I'd be sorry if anyone went down there tonight.

"We've been gone a long time," Connor says. "What if people start to wonder where we are?"

"Everyone's watching a movie," Michael says. "It's fine."

"I agree," Jillian says. "We've come this far. We have to keep going. We have to find out what Agatha wants with us."

The kids grab their flashlights and head for the door.

"Wait," I say. "Let's think about this."

I don't think Agatha was really talking to us tonight. I think Connor was moving the jar. I think he was pretending to be Agatha.

What I don't know is why. Who told him to move the jar? Who told him to spell out GO TO THE FURNACE ROOM?

Here's another thing I don't know:

🐾 Did the message I got from Cat with No Name really come from Agatha or did he just make it up?

It's interesting that the message
I got from Cat was the same message
Jillian was told to record on her tape
recorder. Stay out of the basement.
But we don't know who told Jillian to
record that message, either.

Maybe the kids are right. If we
want to find out what's going on
around here, we may have to go to the
furnace room. We may have to go to
the basement.

There's another loud thunder
crash when we get out into the hall.
Lights in the far hallway flicker.

"I think the stairs over here lead
to the furnace room," Michael says.
He points to the end of the dark
hallway ahead of us.

As we start down the stairs there

is one more loud crash of thunder. This time all the lights in the school go out. We are in total darkness.

"It's okay," Jillian says. "We've got flashlights." She flips hers on. The boys do the same.

All three kids smell very, very nervous.

But we keep going. Down, down, down the stairs.

"You might not be able to get into the furnace room," I warn them when we reach the bottom. "It's probably locked." I remember Maya took the key from the office when she hid the lizards in there.

"Here it is," Michael says, shining his flashlight on a door. "This is the furnace room."

Jillian puts her hand on the doorknob and turns. Surprisingly enough, the door opens. We all step inside.

"Ew," Jillian says. "It's kind of creepy in here."

It's also hot. Hot and loud. Who knew furnaces made so much noise? I smell dirt, dust, mold, spiders, mice, and paint. I can even smell Blue Tongue and the other lizards if I sniff real hard.

Connor and Jillian shine their flashlights all around the room.

"Now what?" Jillian asks.

"I don't know," Connor says.

"Agatha?" Michael calls. "Oh, Agatha! We're here. What do you want us to do next?"

"Did anybody bring the paper and the jar?" Jillian asks, pointing her flashlight at Connor and Michael.

They both squint in the bright light, then shake their heads.

Jillian sighs. "Why not?" she asks Connor. "How are we supposed to talk to her without the paper and the jar?"

We better go back and get it," Michael says. "Otherwise we'll never find out what we have to do next."

"I don't think we need it," Connor says. He takes a deep breath. "Guys, I have to tell you something."

"What?" Jillian and Michael both look at him curiously.

"I, uh, actually got two letters with my flashlight." He reaches into his back pocket and pulls out another piece of paper.

"You did?" Jillian says.

"What does the second one say?" Michael asks, grabbing the paper away from Connor.

"It said I was supposed to move the jar and talk for Agatha," Connor says.

"So you did move the jar," Jillian says.

I knew it!

Connor nods. "I was supposed to get you all to come down here."

"Then what?" Jillian asks. She takes the note from Michael and shines her flashlight on it.

"That's it," Connor says. "Just get you guys to come down here. But

I wasn't supposed to tell you about this second letter. I really don't know why we're down here or what we're supposed to do next."

Connor is telling the truth.

"Maybe we should look around," Jillian says, handing the letter back to Connor. "Maybe there's a clue in here somewhere." She shines her flashlight around the room again.

"I can look for clues, too," I say.

Sniff... sniff... sniff... I stop in front of a wooden chair. There's a paper on the seat of the chair. It has the same chocolate and bubblegum scent on it as the letters and flashlights that Connor, Michael, and Jillian received.

I grab the paper in my mouth and bring it over to Connor.

8
Secret Code

"What have you got there, boy?"
Connor asks, taking the paper from
me.

Michael and Jillian crowd in.
Connor shines his flashlight on the
paper. His forehead wrinkles. "What
in the world—?" he says.

"It's a code," Jillian says.

"How do we crack it?" Michael asks.

"I don't know," Connor says.

"Let me see," I say, nosing my way

in. "Maybe I can crack it."

Okay, maybe not. These are definitely not sight words:

EHMC SGD RDBQDS CNNQ.

SVHRS SGD RBQDVR.

BKHLA SGQNTFG.

ZMC XNT VHKK KDZQM ZKK LX RDBQDSR! —ZFZSGZ

I don't know why Connor, Michael, and Jillian can read other words just fine, but they can't read these words.

"Is it backwards writing?" Jillian asks. "What happens if you try and read the words backwards?"

"Nothing," Connor says. "C-M-H-E isn't a word."

"Are the words scrambled?" Michael asks. "Do we have to unscramble each word?"

"I don't think so," Connor says. "I don't think these are the right letters. Most of the words don't even have any vowels in them."

There has to be a better way to figure out why we're down here than to stare at words that aren't really words. I put my nose to the ground and snifg. I sniff the chair … the furnace … a pile of boxes. So far I don't smell any clues.

"Maybe there's another paper hidden in here somewhere that tells us how to solve that code?" Michael suggests.

"No, I bet we have to figure it out on our own," Connor says.

"How?" Michael asks.

"I don't know," Connor says.

Hey, what's this? I sniff a big metal grate in the wall. I smell that same chocolate and bubblegum scent that I smelled on all the papers and the flashlights.

"Guys, come over here!" I say, wagging my tail.

"What if we replace each letter in the message with the letter that comes before it in the alphabet?" Jillian asks.

"So *E* becomes *D*," Connor says. "*H* becomes *G*. *M* becomes *L*. And *C* becomes *B*."

"D-G-L-B still isn't a word," Michael says.

"Guys! Over here!" I say again. Louder this time.

"Buddy, shh!" Connor says. "We're trying to think."

Connor turns back to the paper. "What if we go the other way? What if we replace each letter with the letter that comes after it in the alphabet?" he says.

"*E* becomes *F*," Jillian says. "*H* becomes *I*. *M* becomes *N*. *C* becomes *D*."

"FIND!" Connor, Michael and Jillian all say at the same time.

"That's a word," Michael cries. "Let's keep going."

I drop my belly to the floor. It's going to take them forever to solve that code. I know that whatever we're looking for, it's on the other side of this grate.

Jillian goes word by word.

"Find … the … secret … door," she says.

"It's right here," I say, sitting back up.

"Twist…the…screws," Connor says.

I look up at the grate. There are screws in each of the corners. "Climb…through," Michael says. He turns to the others. "How do we go forward a letter with *Z*? There are no letters after *Z*."

"Maybe *Z* becomes *A*?" Jillian says.

Like I said: FOREVER! It's taking FOREVER for them to figure out each word.

They say the rest together: "And…you…will…learn…all… my…secrets.—Agatha!"

"So, where's the secret door?"

Michael asks.

"It's here," I say, scratching at the grate. "HERE!"

"Hey, what's that over by Buddy?" Connor asks.

They all hurry over to see.

"Looks like a secret door," Jillian
says with a grin.

"And it's got screws that twist,"
Michael says, his fingers on one of the
top screws.

Connor twists the other top screw.
Jillian twists the two bottom screws.
Then, together, they lift the grate out.

I jump into the hole in the wall.
Whoa! It's some sort of hidden tunnel.
It smells damp and musty in here.
The floor, walls, and ceiling are all
made of concrete. Where does this
tunnel go? I wonder.

"Wait, Buddy!" Connor says,
climbing in after me. He shines his
flashlight around the walls. The
tunnel is tall enough for Connor to
stand in. And wide enough for all

three kids to stand in side by side.

I don't see any secrets," Michael says. "I don't see anything."

"Maybe we have to follow the tunnel and see where it goes," Connor says.

I think Connor is right. Sniff... sniff... "I've got the trail right here," I say, picking up the chocolate and bubblegum scent.

"Follow me!" I dash down the tunnel. The others follow slowly behind me, their flashlights lighting the way.

"Ooooooooooooooo!" a ghostly voice up ahead stops us all in our tracks.

"What was that?" Connor asks.

"I...thinnnk...we have...

viiiiisitors," the ghostly voice continues.

"Oh, goooooood," says another ghostly voice. "I loooooove visitors."

"I-i-is that Agatha?" Jillian whispers.

"I don't know," Michael whispers back.

Sniff… sniff… "No," I say. "I smell humans, not ghosts." Sniff… sniff…

I also smell popcorn. And cookies. And candy. I LOVE popcorn, cookies, and candy. They're my favorite foods!

The tunnel curves and I am moving faster now. "Come on," I call over my shoulder to Connor, Michael, and Jillian.

We are getting closer to the popcorn, the cookies, and the candy. We are also getting closer to the chocolate and bubblegum scent.

All of a sudden, our flashlights light up a group of kids who are sitting on the floor of the tunnel in front of a closet door.

9
The Agatha Society

"Hey, you brought Buddy," one of the kids on the floor says. I go over and let him pet me. Then I sniff at the closed door behind his. I smell dirt ... fertilizer ... gasoline ... tools. Where are we? I wonder. What's on the other side of that door?

"Who are you guys?" Michael asks.

"They're fifth graders," Jillian

says. "This is Tim O'Brien." She points her flashlight at a boy who smells like chocolate, rain, mud, and baseball. The boy squints.

"Tim lives on my street," Jillian goes on. "And that's Alex Shafer." She shines her flashlight on a girl with long, wet hair who smells like chocolate, rain, and mud. "I don't know the other two."

I know one of the others. I know the boy who smells like chocolate, rain, mud, rabbit, and basketball. His name is the same as the girl's: Alex. He's Maya's brother. Hmm. I think I know now where Maya got the idea to hide those lizards in the furnace room. Her brother probably told her about it.

"I'm Alex Lensing," the boy Alex says.

"And I'm Meera Amin," says a girl who smells like chocolate, rain, mud, and bubblegum. Ah-ha! She's the one whose scent I smelled on the grate, and in the tunnel, and on all those papers and flashlights.

"You're probably wondering why we've called you here tonight," Tim says, turning on his flashlight.

"You called us here?" Michael says. He sounds a little disappointed.

"What? Were you thinking Agatha called you here?" Meera says, chomping on her gum. The other fifth graders smirk.

"We are the members of the Agatha Society," Tim says. "We're the ones who invited you here tonight."

"Members of the what?" Connor says.

"The Agatha Society," Tim repeats. "It's a secret club that's been at this school for more than forty years. The only people who know about it are the people who are in it now, the people who have been in it before, and now you guys."

I'm not sure what I think about secret clubs. There used to be another secret club at this school. It was called the Sharks. I remember a boy pulled the fire alarm to get into that club. I hope this isn't that kind of club.

"You have to promise not to tell anyone about this club before we go any further," Meera says. "Do you promise?"

Connor, Michael, and Jillian all look at each other. "I guess. Sure. Okay."

"That doesn't sound very serious," the boy Alex says. "If you're going to join the Agatha Society, you have to take it seriously."

"How do we know we even want to join?" Connor asks. "You haven't told us what the club is or what you do."

Tim, Alex, Alex, and Meera look at each other. "Mostly we sit around and eat candy," the girl Alex says.

"Uh-uh." Meera nudges Alex. "We do other stuff."

"Like what?" Jillian asks.

"We keep the story of Agatha alive," Tim says.

"Was Agatha a real person?" Connor asks.

"Yes," Meera says. "She went to school here a long, long time ago. Her story is written down in here." Meera holds up an old book.

Jillian reaches for the book, but Meera yanks it away. Only full members of the Agatha Society can see the club book."

"What do we have to do to become full members?" Michael asks.

"You've already done most of what you need to do," Tim says. "You were chosen by a current member. You completed the tasks we gave you in your letters. You solved our secret code. And you found your way to our secret hideout. Now all you have to do is take the club oath."

"Before we do that, can you tell us more about the club?" Connor asks. "You must do something besides eat and keep the story of Agatha alive."

"Well, we bring in new members during the fourth grade sleepover." Alex says.

"A long time ago the club used to do random-acts-of-kindness-sorts of things," Meera says. "You know, like give somebody flowers and not say who they're from."

"People were supposed to think they were from Agatha," the girl Alex says.

"There were years the club made ghostly recordings and stuff so people would think the school was haunted," the boy Alex says.

"It's all in the book," Meera says. "Everything the club has ever done is written up in the book."

"There's also a list of all the people who have ever been members of the club in the book," Tim says. "There are some very surprising names on that list." He wiggles his eyebrows.

"Yeah? Like who?" Michael asks.

Meera hugs the book tight to her chest. "You can't know that until you're an official member of the club," she says.

"So what do you say?" Tim asks. "Do you want to join the best club at this school?"

"Yes! Yes! For sure!" Connor,

Michael, and Jillian say.

"Okay, then," Tim says. "Come join our circle."

The fifth graders all stand up and make room for the fourth graders. I stay back out of the circle.

"Raise your right hand and repeat after me," Tim says, holding up his right hand.

Connor, Michael and Jillian all raise their right hands.

"I, state your name," Tim says.

"I, Connor Keene—"

"Michael Ford—"

"Jillian Sinclair—"

"Do solemnly swear to keep all the secrets of the Agatha Society," Tim says.

"Do solemnly swear to keep all the secrets of the Agatha Society," Connor, Michael, and Jillian repeat, their hands still raised.

"I now pronounce you members of the Agatha Society," Tim says.

The other fifth graders clap.

Connor, Michael, and Jillian all grin at each other.

"Cool," Michael says.

Tim reaches into his pocket and pulls out three shiny objects. Keys.

He hands one to each of the fourth graders.

"What are these for?" Connor asks, eying the key in his hand.

"You know that old shed that's in the back of the school?" the boy Alex says.

"Yeah," Connor says.

The boy Alex puts his hand on the door behind him. "That's what's on the other side of this door. It's how we get in here for meetings. Your key unlocks the shed. Once you're in the shed, you can get into the tunnel, and eventually into the furnace room and the rest of the school."

"Do any of the teachers know kids have these keys?" Connor asks.

"Does my mom?"

"Nope," says Meera. "And we're going to keep it that way."

"How do you get into the school from the tunnel?" Jillian asks. "Doesn't somebody have to be in the school to untwist the screws on the grate?"

"Not if the screws aren't in very tight," Tim says. "You should be able to kick the grate in. And voilà! You're in the school."

"Cool," Michael says.

"We hold all our meetings right here in the tunnel," the girl Alex says.

"If you ever tell anyone about the club or its secrets, you'll be kicked out," Meera warns.

"Don't worry," Michael says. "We

know how to keep a secret. Don't we, guys?"

"Yes! Of course." Connor and Jillian nod their heads.

"Good," Meera says. She brings the big book over to them and opens it up. Connor, Michael, and Jillian gaze at it. I try and look, too, but it's all writing. No pictures.

Tim reaches into his pocket, pulls out a pen, and hands it to Jillian. "Now you guys have to sign the book."

I watch as Jillian, Connor, and Michael all write their names.

"So who else has been a member of this club?" Michael asks, paging back through the book. "You said there were some surprising names in here, but so far I don't recognize any of them."

The fifth graders all grin knowingly at one another.

"Keep going," Alex the girl says. "All the way back to the first name on the list."

Connor and Jillian peer over Michael's shoulder. Connor's eyes just about pop out of his head. He points to something on the page and Jillian and Michael both gasp.

"Allan Poe?" Jillian says, wide-eyed. "Is that … Mr. Poe? Our janitor?"

The fifth graders keep on grinning.

"Mr. Poe wasn't just a member of the club," Tim says. "He's the one who started the whole thing!"

10
Case Closed

"Does Mr. Poe know we have these keys?" Jillian asks.

"I don't think so," the boy Alex says. "If you read the book you'll see the club only got keys about eight years ago."

"Cool," Michael says.

"We'll meet here again next Friday at five o'clock," Tim says. He opens the door behind him and I try and push my nose inside.

"No, Buddy," Connor calls. "You're coming with us."

"Fine," I say. Maybe Connor will bring me to his next meeting and I'll be able to go in that shed then.

"Remember, don't put the screws back on the grate very tight," Meera says. "Otherwise we won't be able to get into the school if we need to."

The kids all say good-bye. Then the fifth graders leave through the door to the shed, and the fourth graders and I trot back down the tunnel the way we came. Connor and Jillian's flashlights light the way.

"The Agatha Society," Jillian says. "That is so cool!"

"I wonder why they picked us to join?" Connor asks.

"Who cares why?" Michael says. "I'm just glad they did."

We climb back into the furnace room. Michael and Jillian put the grate in place while Connor holds the flashlight.

"Ready to go back to the sleepover?" Connor says.

"Sure," Michael replies, opening the door. There are lights on in the basement hallway now.

"Looks like the electricity is back on," Jillian say.

"Good," Connor says. "Then we don't need our flashlights anymore."

Yes, but I don't think the lights were on down here before the electricity went out. Why are they on now?

We march up the stairs. There are

a lot of lights on up here, too. I know these lights weren't on before.

Hey, I hear people calling me from another part of the school. "Buddy! Where are you, Buddy?"

"Connor? Michael? Jillian?"

"Uh oh," Connor says. "Do you think people are looking for us?"

"We're here!" I yell, bounding toward the voices.

I round a corner and, wow, it's like a party! There are so many humans here. Fourth grade humans and full-grown humans like Mr. Poe and Mrs. Warner. And they are all petting me.

"Look, Mrs. Keene," says one of the kids. "We found Buddy."

"And here comes Jillian, Connor, and Michael, too," says another kid.

I break away from the kids who are petting me and race toward Mom. She gives me a little pat on the head, but her eyes are fixed on Connor, Michael, and Jillian.

"Where have you three been?" Mom asks, standing up tall. She looks worried. And a little bit mad. Connor bites his lip. Jillian lowers her eyes. Michael grinds his toe against the floor.

"Connor?" Mom folds her arms. "I asked you a question. Everyone's been looking for you."

"Uh … we were in the music room," Connor says in a small voice. It's true. Connor, Michael and Jillian were in the music room. But there's a lot more to the story than that.

"Why were you in the music room?" Mom asks. "Didn't I say that the music room was off limits?"

"We were ... looking for ghosts," Michael says.

"Did you find any?" Mr. Poe asks with a wink of his eye.

Michael starts to smile, but Jillian nudges him.

"Don't encourage them, Mr. Poe," Mom says. "There are no such things as ghosts!"

"We're sorry, Mom," Connor says. "We know we weren't supposed to be in the music room. We just wanted to see if we could figure out what Michael saw in there earlier."

"Well, I hope the three of you will follow directions the rest of the

night," Mom says.

We all troop back to the library. Along the way, Mom leans over and says to Connor, "We'll talk about this some more when we get home."

Connor groans.

We pass the main door to the school and a flash of gray outside catches my eye.

I stop. Is that ... Cat with No Name?

No, it can't be. Cats don't like to be out in the rain. I peer closer. It sure looks like Cat with No Name. He's all huddled up against the door. I let all the humans go on without me, then I pad over to the door.

"What are you doing here?" I ask Cat. I actually feel a little bit bad for him being stuck out in the rain.

Cat lifts his chin. "I'm waiting for Agatha," he says coolly. "We have an appointment."

"Ha!" I say. "There is no Agatha."

"Really?" Cat says, blinking his eyes. "Are you sure about that?"

"Yes!" I say. "There ars no such things as ghosts. All that stuff about Agatha is just a story that's been passed down through this club called the Agatha Society. But you probably already know that."

For some reason, Cat seems to know everything. I don't know where he gets his information.

"You probably know that the club members meet in this tunnel that you can only get to from the shed out back or through the furnace room in the basement," I go on. "That's probably why you told me to stay out of the basement. You didn't want me to find all that out."

Cat blinks his eyes again.

"You may know practically everything there is to know," I tell Cat. "But that doesn't mean you can make a fool out of me. Not today!"

It feels so good to finally stand up to Cat with no Name.

"Well, there's always tomorrow," Cat says. Then he turns and walks out into the rainy night, his tail held high.

I skip back to the library. The fourth graders are getting settled in their sleeping bags. I go over and find a nice spot between Connor and Michael. I rest my head on Connor's stomach and my tail on Michael's leg. Mom turns on another movie, and one by one, all the kids drift off to sleep.

I guess I solved the Case of the School Ghost. But I have a feeling we haven't seen the last of Agatha. Or the last of the Agatha Society.

About Dori Hillestad Butler

Dori Hillestad Butler is the author of more than thirty books for children, including picture books, chapter books, and middle grade novels. Her middle grade novels *Sliding Into Home; Trading Places with Tank Talbott; Do You Know the Monkey Man;* and *The Truth About Truman School* have been on children's choice award lists in sixteen different states. She's been a ghostwriter for several popular series, including Sweet Valley Twins and The Boxcar Children.

Her Edgar® Award–winning series, The Buddy Files, is a chapter book series about a school therapy dog who solves mysteries. Dori and her dog, Mouse, are a registered pet partner team in Coralville, Iowa, where they participate in a program that promotes reading with dogs.

She grew up in southern Minnesota and now lives in Coralville, Iowa, with her husband, son, dog, and cat.

Praise for The Buddy Files:

"With twists and turns, humor, and a likable canine character, this series should find a wide fan base."—*Booklist*

"Readers should be drawn in by Buddy's exuberant voice." —*Publishers Weekly*

"Sweet and suspenseful." —*Kirkus Reviews*

Now available as e-books at your favorite online retailer!

The Buddy Files

He's a dog. He's also a detective!

The Buddy Files

THE CASE of THE LOST BOY

Dori Hillestad Butler

pictures by Jeremy Tugeau

WINNER!
2011 EDGAR® AWARD
FOR BEST JUVENIL
MYSTERY

Zapato Power: The Adventures of Freddie Ramos

One day Freddie Ramos comes home from school and finds a strange box just for him. What's inside?

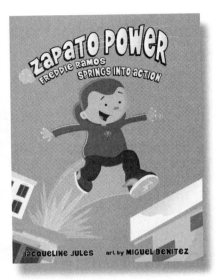

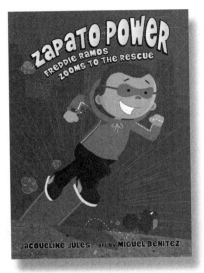

Mermaid Mysteries

There's a mystery to be solved—and the young mermaid detectives are on the case!

VAMPIRE SCHOOL

Sink your teeth into the
Vampire School series.